ROUTINE MURDER

COZY MYSTERY TAILS OF ALASKA, BOOK 4

PATTI BENNING

SUMMER PRESCOTT BOOKS PUBLISHING

Angie Seaver bit her lip as she carefully folded an omelette in half. It was *almost* perfect, just a smidge crooked, but it hadn't broken, so that was something. It was stuffed full of green onions, cheese, tomatoes, and spinach leaves. It actually looked delicious, and she felt a pinch in her stomach, reminding her that she hadn't eaten anything besides a package of instant oatmeal since early that morning, almost five hours ago. *I'm going to have to take a break soon,* she thought. *I've been spending all morning feeding everyone but myself.*

She slid the near-perfect omelette onto a plate next to a serving of hash browns and added a dollop of sour cream beside it. She picked up the paper the order was scribbled on and double checked it. When she was satisfied, she picked up the other three plates and placed them all on a large tray around a carafe of syrup.

She took the plates out into the dining area, looking around. It didn't take her long to spot the four people to whom the food belonged. Three of them were regulars; they came in at ten a.m. on the dot every Tuesday morning. The older couple, the Franklins, had been supporters of the diner since before it had even opened. Mr. Franklin had granted Angie's father the loan he had needed to open the business all those years ago. He had been a loyal customer ever since, and he, along with his wife, Shirley, and his best friend, Ronald, were well-known at Lost Bay Burgers. Today, however, there was someone new sitting with them. A young woman, who looked like she was probably in her late teens, was sitting next to Shirley, scrunched into the far corner of the booth with her feet up on the cushion and her phone inches from her face. She was squinting at the screen, ignoring the conversation going on around her.

Angie felt a twinge of curiosity, then shook her head, silently laughing at herself. When exactly had she gotten so interested in the lives of the diner's regulars? Over the past couple of months, she had lost the big city habit of ignoring everyone else. She had become familiar, even friendly, with a lot of the diner's patrons. They chatted with her, shared parts of their lives with her, and she had to admit she liked the fact that half of the people who stopped by seemed to know her name.

She made her way over to the table and handed the orders out, calling out the dishes as she did so.

"Does everything look right?" she asked.

There were affirmative nods all around.

"Can I get you guys refills on any of your drinks?"

"I'll have another coffee," Mrs. Franklin said. "Decaf, this time, if that's all right."

"Of course. I'll be right back out with that."

She turned to leave, but paused when the woman spoke again. "Oh, Angie, I wanted to introduce you to my granddaughter, Madison. Madison, this lovely young lady is Angie. She's Rod Seaver's daughter. You know him, he owns the diner."

"I don't know him, Grandma," the younger woman said. "But that's cool, I guess. Working for your dad. It can't be too hard."

"He can be pretty tough," Angie said, giving the young woman a polite smile. "He doesn't go easy on me just because I'm his daughter. I do like working here, though. It's nice to meet you, I hope you enjoy your stay here."

"She's staying with us for the rest of the summer," Mrs. Franklin said, beaming over at her granddaughter, who had already turned her attention back to her cell phone. "She just graduated from high school, and she's going off to college this fall. I'm so happy we get to have her here for a few months before then."

"Well, I'm sure you'll have a lovely time with her this summer," Angie said. She turned her attention back to the younger woman. "Lost Bay may be small, but don't give up on it quite yet. It's a good little town, and there's a lot to do if you know where to look. You're always welcome to stop in here and ask for directions if you need to."

"I'm sure I'll be able to find my way around," Madison mumbled. "But, thanks."

Angie returned to the kitchen, focusing on getting the next few orders out. While the Franklins might be honored guests at the diner, all of the other customers were equally as important. She couldn't stay and chat, not that she was really complaining. Mrs. Franklin was one of those people who seemed to never run out of things to say.

A good twenty minutes passed before she got the chance to check in on the Franklins again. When she did, their food was nearly gone, and Mr. Franklin's seat was empty.

"Can I get you guys anything else?" she asked as she started to clear the table.

"No, thanks," Ronald, the family friend who often joined them, said. "We're all heading to my house after this and I've got some strawberries and cream waiting."

"That's right," Mrs. Franklin said. "We are going to show Madison his weather watching equipment. He's an amateur weather man. He has his own show on the internet and everything." She began animatedly telling her granddaughter all about it.

Angie piled some plates on top of one other and quickly took them into the kitchen, not wanting to interrupt the older woman's conversation. She rested the plates near the dishwasher and then went back out for a second load, only to be waylaid by a hand on her shoulder as she passed by the men's restroom.

She jumped, but it was just Mr. Franklin. He looked a bit paler than usual, and she could tell by the way he was putting his weight on her shoulder that he was unsteady on his feet.

"Are you doing all right, sir?" she asked, suddenly concerned for him.

"Do you see them?"

"See what?"

"The people, watching me. They're lined up in the windows. Don't you see them? They've been following me all day."

Angie felt a chill as she looked toward the diner's windows. There was no one there, of course, but it didn't help the uneasy feeling that settled into her gut.

"I'm sorry, Mr. Franklin, but I don't see anyone."

"They're going to kill me," he said softly. "It's just a matter of time now. They're hiding in plain sight. No one else sees them, but I do. I know they're out to get me."

He released her shoulder and walked shakily back to his table, leaving Angie to stare after him. She wasn't sure what she was supposed to do. Should she say something to his wife? But no, Mrs. Franklin was standing up and giving him a kiss on the cheek, gently guiding him down into his seat. She seemed extra attentive toward him, and Angie got the feeling that she knew perfectly well that her husband's mind was beginning to slip.

"Well, I hope the four of you have a great day," she said, forcing a bit of cheer into her voice as she picked up the last of the dishes and grabbed the money they had left to pay for the check. "I'll be right back with your change."

"Keep the change, Angie, dear." Mrs. Franklin patted her hand. "You have a nice day, too. Don't neglect to go outside. We're supposed to be getting lovely weather this week, I wouldn't want you to waste it all cooped up in here."

Angie thanked her for the tip and pocketed the money. "I'll try to get some sun," she promised. "I'll see you next week. It was nice to meet you, Madison."

The young woman gave her a ghost of a nod, and then the group got up and began to leave. Angie hurried back to the kitchen to deposit the dishes, then she counted out the money, recorded her tip on the roster by the register, and returned to the kitchen, fighting back a yawn. She didn't think she would ever stop feeling a dip in energy in the middle of the day. She only had a couple of hours left in her shift, but once it was over, she was planning on going out with Maggie, grabbing a cup of coffee, and waiting around until Maggie's son, Joshua, got done with school. The plan was to spend an hour or two exploring some of the closer nature trails. It sounded great the evening before, but right now all she wanted to do was take a nap.

A voice jolted her out of her thoughts, and she managed to shake some of the tiredness away.

"I can do those," Theo, one of the younger employees said, reaching for the dishes she had set down before she had a chance to start washing them. "You should've let me bus the table. It's my job to do all that. You're supposed to focus on the cooking. You're nearly as bad as your dad is."

She blinked, then gave a small chuckle. She was glad that Theo was finally getting more comfortable with her. When she first started working there, he had acted as though she was an extension of her father. The fact that he was finally able to joke around with her was a good thing, as far she was concerned.

"I feel bad leaving them all for you," she admitted. "I was standing right there. I might as well take the dishes back with me. The table still needs to be cleaned off, though."

"I'll take care of that, then I'll come back and do these dishes. I hate just standing around and twiddling my thumbs, and I'm not trained to work the grill yet, so if you do the dishes, where does that leave me? I might have to do something horrible like clean the woman's bathroom." He gave an over-exaggerated look of horror.

"Ah, yes. That would be true desperation." Angie grabbed the wire grill brush from where it was hanging on the wall. "I'll leave the dishes for you since you asked so nicely. The grill needs to be cleaned anyway before we start getting more of the lunch crowd in. I swear, my dad really knows how to hire people. I still don't know how he managed to find employees that actually want to be kept busy all day."

Theo grabbed a spray bottle and a rag from the counter. "Keeping busy makes the time go faster," he said with a shrug. "Plus, don't tell anyone, but I actually like doing all this, keeping the restaurant clean and stuff. It's relaxing. A lot more relaxing than cooking. If I start letting you do my job, I might have to do yours. And trust me, you do not want me working the grill yet."

"I think you'd pick it up pretty quickly," she said. "But getting your first grill lesson ten minutes before the lunch rush starts probably isn't the best idea. Hop to it, we should both get our jobs done soon. We're going to be busy again before we know it."

"Right, sorry," he said, looking chagrined. "The tables will be sparkling before you know it, Ms. – I mean, Angie."

She smiled as she watched him leave the kitchen. There were definitely moments when he still thought of her as the boss's daughter, rather than just another employee, but he was getting there. Until she was officially in a management position, she wanted everyone else to treat her just like they treated each other. She wanted to be one of them, instead of only being seen as her father's daughter.

2

Maggie stopped by the diner shortly before Angie's shift was over. She ordered a diet soda and sat at the counter, sipping it while she watched Angie get ready to leave. She seemed to be enjoying the sight of her friend scurrying back and forth, carrying orders, printing out checks, and counting change. Angie stuck out her tongue at her as she rushed by, knowing that her friend was taunting her on purpose.

Maggie had been her best friend growing up, but the two of them had grown apart once they graduated high school and left town, going their separate ways. Both of them had returned within months of each other and had picked up the friendship almost as if it had never left off. Sometimes Angie got a strange sense of déjà vu. It seemed like almost nothing in the town had changed at all, including her relationships with the people who lived there. She was used to the fast paced, always changing life of Southern California, and moving back here was definitely an entirely different experience. A cold one. Winter, it seemed, would never fully let go of the small town. For someone who loved hot, dry weather and sunny days at the beach, she had certainly chosen an interesting place to live.

"So, how's the job?" her friend asked when Angie finally was able to take a breather. Betty had just walked in, which meant that her shift was officially over. "I know you worked this weekend. Did you get a chance to hang out with Malcolm and his kids again?"

"If by hang out, you mean serve them silly pancakes on Saturday morning, then yes," Angie said. "I already told you, Mags, we're taking things slow. The day he introduces me to his kids as his girlfriend, or whatever he decides to call me in front of them, is the day that our relationship goes from something fun and casual to something serious. I completely understand him not wanting his kids exposed to every single woman he dates."

"And by 'all the women', you mean you and only you," Maggie said. "He's not really playing the field. Trust me, it's a small town. You would know."

Angie rolled her eyes good-naturedly. "True. But you know what I mean. Malcolm and I are really good friends, and even if we break up, we will still be in each other's lives, but neither of us is really ready for a major commitment right now. For one thing, I don't know how long I'm going to be in town. It's all kind of up in the air. I mean, my dad wants me to take over the restaurant, but I'm not one-hundred percent sure that's what I want to do with my life. What if I change my mind in two months? And Malcolm hasn't been divorced long, he's not exactly ready to jump into a serious relationship right away. We're happy with how things are."

"If you say so," Maggie said. "I guess that's what matters. I just think the two of you go so well together."

"We do," Angie said with a smile. "And who knows, maybe we'll still be together in sixty years." She thought of the Franklins, who had been together for longer than she had been alive. "But it is also possible that we might decide to go our separate ways, relationship-wise, next week. I mean, I don't think it's very likely, but it's possible. I don't want to become a major part of his kids' lives just to disappear after a few weeks or months. That wouldn't be fair to them."

"You're right," her friend said. Angie thought from the expression on her face that she was probably thinking of her own son. She and Joshua's father had gotten divorced only a few months ago, and Maggie was still figuring out how to be a single parent. "Sorry. I'll stop pressuring you."

"It's fine," Angie said honestly. "I know you're mostly just teasing. It's nice having someone to talk to about all of this. It's kind of weird talking about it with my mom, since she's known Malcolm longer than I have."

Maggie snorted. "I can imagine. That must be strange."

"It definitely is, sometimes. The worst part is, there have been a few mornings when Malcolm came over to help my dad with the dogs or ask him something, and I didn't know he was going to be there. Thanks to that time I stepped out the front door to let Petunia outside, and he was in the front yard, he has already seen me in my pajamas with no makeup and my hair sticking up all crazy. I suppose the fact that he's still attracted to me is somewhat promising. I'm not quite sure I like the feeling of sharing my boyfriend with both of my parents, though."

"Well, thanks for that disturbing image," her friend

said. She drained the last of her soda and stood up. "I need some real caffeine, that soda was just to tide me over. You ready to go?"

"Sure thing. Let me just say goodbye to Theo and Betty. I'll be right back out."

A few minutes later the two of them got into Maggie's car. It was a smoother ride than the old truck Angie was driving. She had left the nearly new car she was leasing down in California, and she missed it like a missing limb. Driving a vehicle that was so old was not something she would ever get used to.

Frozen Grounds was just down the street from the diner. It was one of the newest businesses in town, and was one of the only visible changes to Main Street. As far as Angie was concerned, it was a good one. The coffee shop had state-of-the-art machines, including an espresso machine that made the best drinks that Angie had ever had in her entire life.

And she was an avid coffee fanatic, so that said something.

She and Maggie each ordered a latte and claimed a small table by the window, which was warmed by the sunlight. It was a nice day, as far as early spring in Alaska went, and it promised to be a beautiful summer, short though it would be. Angie was beginning to feel antsy, which was something she felt every spring. She wanted to organize her books, clean the house, and take an inventory of her life. The only problem was, she wasn't sure she would like what she found. Here she was, thirty years old, living with her parents and working in the family restaurant. Granted, she had only moved back to take care of her ailing mother, and she enjoyed working at the diner. But still, it wasn't exactly where she had envisioned herself being back when she had first set out on her own.

"You okay?" Maggie asked, raising an eyebrow. "You've got a sort of sad expression on your face."

"Sorry," Angie said, laughing and shaking her head. "I was just wondering what my twenty-year-old self would think if she could see me now."

"I think she would be pretty happy."

"You do?" Angie asked. It was her turn to raise her eyebrows.

"I do," her friend said, sipping her coffee. "I mean, you had a good job and a successful life with lots of friends down in California, then you decided to leave all that behind and move up here to make amends with your parents. You did the right thing, and I think that would have mattered to twenty-year-old Angie."

"I don't know," Angie said. She tapped her fingers on the table, looking out the window. "What am I doing here, long term, Mags? Am I really going to spend the rest of my life waiting tables and making burgers?"

"Do you think less of your dad for spending his life doing that?"

"No, of course not. He's successful and hard-working and loves his job. There's nothing wrong with any of that. I guess I just feel like it's different for a woman. I have to... prove myself more, somehow. When my dad tells people he owns a restaurant, most people think it's cool, and that it's a sign he's a hard worker and earned what he has. He built the place from the ground up, after all. I just feel like if I tell people I manage my father's burger joint, they will think 'is that all she did with her life?' I keep feeling like I should achieve more."

"You can still do anything you want," Maggie said. "Are you unhappy working at the diner?"

"Not at all," Angie said. "I love it there. It's so laid-back, and everyone feels like family. It feels... comfortable."

"So, if you're happy, who cares what anyone else thinks? Really, most people don't even care what your job is. What matters is who you are, not what you do. Do you look down on Betty for having worked there all those years?"

"Not at all," Angie said. "She's an amazing woman. She's had an awesome life, too. She has traveled all over the world and raised a family pretty much on her own after her husband passed away. She loves her job, she has the most adorable house, and she lived her life exactly the way she wanted to."

"Why are you trying to hold yourself to a different standard then?" Maggie asked.

Angie raised her hands in a gesture of surrender.

"Okay, okay. I get it. I'm just being silly. I guess all this talking about my relationship with Malcolm kind of made me wonder where I'll be in another ten years. I mean, I would like to have kids one day. I want a husband, my own house, all of that. I don't want to just get stuck living with my parents forever, even though I know my mom needs me now. They're at a tough time in their lives but I think my dad is planning on moving into retirement within the next couple of years, and after that I should be able to start living more of my own life again since he will be able to spend more time with her."

"See? It will all work out. Just relax and try to enjoy where you're at now. You're not in a huge hurry. We're both still young, there's no need to worry about all of this too much."

Angie nodded. "You're right. I shouldn't worry so much. I think I might just be going a little bit stir crazy."

"I know the feeling," Maggie said. "I love Lost Bay and all, but sometimes I feel like the entire town is stuck in a giant rut. Poor Josh is feeling the same way. He keeps talking about all of the different activities he wants to do once school lets out. I just don't know how I'm going to be able to drive him to them all and still keep up my hours at the police station."

"Well, I'm happy to give him a ride if I'm able," Angie said. "It wouldn't be any trouble, especially if I'm already heading into work. I can just leave home a little earlier."

"Would you really do that? I would appreciate it so much. It's going to be hard this summer with him and with how much I'm working. In a couple of years, he will be able to stay home on his own, but I'm just not comfortable with it right now. He's only a kid, and he can't take care of himself all day while I'm working. I know he's a good kid, but he is also smart, and he likes pushing boundaries. I don't even want to think about what kind of trouble he could get himself into."

"The two of you will figure it out," Angie said. "You have a great relationship. I really wish I had a similar one with my parents. I mean, it's not like we had a terrible relationship when I was younger, but we definitely weren't as close as you and Josh are."

"Well, I guess that's what you get when you're raising a kid alone. I just can't do everything that two people can do, so he ends up picking up some of the slack himself. It's not perfect, but like you said, we're making it work. And even though it's hard sometimes, I wouldn't trade my relationship with my son for anything. He makes everything worth it."

Angie nodded. "I don't know if I can fully understand that, since I haven't had kids myself, but I think I get it. I know Malcolm feels the same way, even though he doesn't have full custody of his kids. It really is life-changing, isn't it?"

Her friend nodded. "Completely."

The coffee shop door opened, and Angie looked over toward it reflexively. The young woman who walked into the building looked familiar, but it took Angie a moment to place her. It was the Franklins' granddaughter, Madison. She had her cell phone pressed to her ear and seemed completely focused on the conversation she was having.

"Yeah, it's terrible here," she was saying loudly. "I get phone service in like one, twenty square-foot area on Main Street. Thank goodness the best service is right by a coffee shop. My grandparents are busy shopping at some antique store with one of their friends. At least they didn't try to make me follow them around inside that dusty place. This town is dead, Devon. I'm telling you I don't know how I'm going to stay sane here."

She paused, walking up to the counter and frowning at the menu. "Hold on, I've got to order." She turned her attention to the barista. "Yeah, I'll have the vanilla latte with a double shot of espresso, please. Thanks."

She handed the woman behind the counter a few bills, then turned her attention back to her cell phone.

"Everything is so run down here. We went out to eat at a diner this morning, and I swear, it looks like it's right out of the 80s." There was a pause, while whoever was on the other line spoke. "Well, yeah, the food was good, but it was so fattening. I swear I'm going to gain twenty pounds in the first month. I'm already up two. I wish I could just go back home, but Mom says as long as Grandma and Grandpa are willing to take me, I'm stuck here. Something about forming a relationship before it's too late. I think she just wants their money. I mean, I do too. But it's not like they're going to drop dead and leave it all to us tomorrow."

She grabbed her coffee, and walked over to a table not too far from Angie and Maggie. The two older women exchanged a glance, and then Maggie unabashedly turned her attention back toward the younger woman. Angie felt a small spur of guilt for eavesdropping, but the young woman wasn't exactly being quiet. It would be impossible to ignore her.

"Yeah, I miss you too, Devon. I'll try to get home soon, I promise. My grandparents are going to somewhere later today with one of their friends, and I'm being dragged along. I'll try to get on the computer this evening, though. Tell everyone I miss them. Bye."

She drank her coffee, scrolling down her phone screen and seeming like she was trying to pretend the world around her didn't exist. Maggie was looking quite amused, and nodded her head at the clock. "As entertaining as that was, Josh's school just got out. Let's go pick him up, then head out to the trails. I hope he never ends up with an attitude like that girl."

"I'm sure she's got some hidden depths," Angie said, tossing her empty coffee cup in the garbage can as they left the shop. "I met her at the diner earlier, and her grandparents seem thrilled to have her. She obviously doesn't want to be here, and that's got to make everything that much worse."

"You've got a point. Still, I think that spending some time here will be good for her. She needs to slow down and enjoy life a little bit."

3

Thursday morning was dreary. Angie woke up to the sound of rain pattering on the steel roof. She wasn't looking forward to driving to work in the dark, wet weather, but she didn't have much of a choice. She took her time getting ready, sipping a glass of orange juice and enjoying a bowl of oatmeal, deciding to forgo the coffee until she got to the diner. She didn't know what it was; even though her parents' coffee was the exact same brand they used at the diner, it never tasted quite as good.

She could have sworn that the rain started falling harder when she stepped outside. She tucked her coat around herself, getting into the truck as quickly as possible and slamming the door shut. The drive to town was long and unpleasant, but at least inside the diner it was warm, dry, and quiet, other than for the pitter patter of the rain on the roof. The coffee maker gurgled while she stumbled through her morning routine. Betty arrived only a few minutes after she did, and they finished the opening routine quickly.

"Angie, is everything all right?"

Angie jerked when she heard Betty speak. She realized that she had been staring at the coffee maker for nearly a full minute without moving. It had fallen silent; the coffee was ready.

"Just tired," Angie said as she reached for a clean mug to pour the hot liquid into. "I feel like a zombie this morning. I just want to curl up in front of a fire with a book, or maybe a good movie."

"It is that sort of day," Betty said. "The good news is, the rain will melt the rest of the snow."

"Wonderful, I'll be able see all of the mud and dead grass instead of the snow. Quite an improvement."

The older woman chuckled, shaking her head. Angie stirred in creamer and sugar and sipped her coffee, finally feeling more like herself. "I know I've said this before, but I really miss the weather in Southern California. It's warm, dry, and summer lasts there as long as winter does here."

"Alaska has its own beauty," Betty said. "Not everyone can see it, but those who do are lucky."

"I do think it's a beautiful state," Angie admitted. "I'm just grumpy because I skipped out on coffee earlier this morning and the rain makes everything humid and damp. I'll try to cheer up a bit."

"The mornings will be easier when the sun is up to

greet you," Betty said, tying an apron around herself. "I don't particularly enjoy waking up in the dark and the rain either. Nothing we can do about it, though. Let's move onto happier topics. Do you have any plans for this weekend?"

"I'm probably going to see Maggie and Josh again," Angie said. "And I have a date with Malcolm on Friday night. It's been a pretty busy week, so I don't want to schedule too much for myself. I'd like some downtime. My mom and I want to tackle cleaning out part of the attic, too. How about you?"

"I might have my son coming up to visit me with his family," the older woman said. "It's been a while since I've seen them, so I'm really looking forward to it."

"I hope they make it up," she said. "That would be nice for you."

"It depends on the weather. If it's too bad, they'll have to come another weekend. I'm not having them risk themselves just to come see me, even though I miss them a ridiculous amount. That's just how it is for parents, though. You never stop missing your kids when they leave the house." She chuckled. "Well, the peace and quiet is nice for the first few years, I won't deny that."

"I think it's great that your son and his family come to visit you," Angie said. "I regret staying away from home for so long. I think my mom and I are closer than ever, and I'm getting to know my father better as well. My brother mentioned he's going to try to visit more too. It's nice that my family is getting closer again. None of us will ever stop missing my sister, but I think we're finally starting to heal."

"That's how it's supposed to be. You'll never forget her, but over time all of the sharp edges will begin to dull," the other woman said somberly. She patted the back of Angie's hand gently.

The dreary weather seemed to encourage thoughts about her sister. Her mind was on the past as she and Betty unlocked the front door and flipped over the open sign. Her sister had passed away in a car accident a decade ago. The youngest of the three siblings, her death had hit everyone hard. It had been the catalyst that had broken the family apart, and Angie knew that none of them would ever really get over it. It had taught her a lot about grief, and at a relatively young age. She would never, ever stop missing her little sister. She knew that to the core of her being. But she was gradually getting used to that feeling. Just like Betty had said, the years had softened it. Sometimes she felt guilty for not thinking about her more often. Wasn't thinking about her the least she could do?

There was one customer already waiting in the parking lot when she and Betty opened the diner. Angie hurried into the kitchen to get them a clean mug and to grab the pot of regular coffee, pushing her dwellings on the past aside for the time being. The early morning customers were her favorites, and this time of day was special to her. The quiet and the routine helped boost her spirits.

The customer held on to the warm coffee mug like her life depended on it. She was older, maybe in her later fifties or sixties. She looked miserable.

"Are there any decent hotels in this town??" she asked when Angie brought her her food. "I've been staying in a cheap motel since Monday night, and I just can't take it anymore. I'm staying longer for a funeral, and I'm willing to pay for a place with a comfortable bed."

"There's a bed and breakfast a few miles outside of town," Angie suggested. "You might want to try there. We don't have any major hotels here, unfortunately."

"All right. I'll give it a try. Do you have the number?"

Angie hurried to find the number, but by the time she had dug it out of the Rolodex her father kept by the phone, the woman had paid for the meal and left. Frowning, Angie left the card by the register, in case she came back.

Despite the rainy weather, quite a few people straggled in that morning. Angie spent the early hours, her favorite time to work at the diner, waiting and bussing tables, greeting her morning regulars, and serving pot after pot of coffee. Later that morning, when the early morning regulars were gone and the rowdier breakfast crowd was beginning to arrive, she switched places with Betty and spent a couple of hours making food almost as quickly as the orders came in. Bacon, waffles, pancakes, and eggs of every kind imaginable; bowls of fresh fruit and oatmeal, and the occasional breakfast sandwich. She put her all into every dish, only to hand it off to Betty before turning her focus to the next one. Later in the morning, she switched gears to soup, salads, and sandwiches, even though breakfast was popular all day. The sheer number of different dishes she knew how to make from rote memory surprised her. It helped that none of the food was very complex. It was all simple, hearty, good tasting food.

There was a lull between the breakfast rush and the lunch rush, and Angie spent it washing the pile of dishes that had gotten backlogged during the busy morning. Betty wasn't about to complain when she did the dishes, and Angie found the easy, mindless job soothing after spending all of the morning cooking. When Betty went out to get the newspaper, Angie hardly paid her any mind. The small-town newspaper was filled with advertisements, personal announcements, and the occasional news story of import. Angie rarely read it, her father and Betty both loved it.

The older woman came back in and mentioned that she was going to take a short break. She picked up the coffee pot, poured some into a mug, and sipped it black. Angie gave a distracted nod, and was so focused on the dishes that she nearly forgot Betty was there until she heard the other woman say, "Oh, dear."

"Is something wrong?" Angie asked, still only half paying attention as she scrubbed a particularly stubborn pan.

"You know the Franklins?"

"The regulars that come in every Tuesday morning? I do. I actually chatted with them a bit this week. They have their granddaughter staying with them for a few months. Why, did something happen?"

"Philip Franklin passed away Tuesday night," Betty said.

Her stomach dropped. "Really? That's horrible. Let me see."

She shut off the water and quickly dried her hands, turning to take the paper from Betty. She read through the obituary section, her heart sinking.

Philip Franklin passed away of natural causes Tuesday evening. He is remembered by his wife, Shirley Franklin, his sister Zelda Hamilton, and his granddaughter, Madison Franklin. The funeral will be held on Sunday at 11 AM. All are welcome to attend.

She handed the paper back to Betty, who looked at the announcement again and shook her head sadly. "The funeral is Sunday. I'm going to have to tell my son to come up next weekend instead of this one. Philip's wife is a dear friend of mine, I need to be there for her."

"I should tell my dad," Angie said. "He's going to want to go as well. I should probably go too, which means we will have to see if Theo or Grace will be able to work that shift at the diner."

She had avoided funerals like the plague ever since her sister's death, finding them dark reminders of that terrible day when they had buried the youngest of the Seavers. She would go to this one, though. Not

43

only would it look odd if the rest of her family went and she didn't, but she'd gotten to know the Franklins pretty well over the past few months and the elderly man's death saddened her. Of course, she knew that it must be nothing compared to what his family felt. They must be devastated.

4

Angie took the news of Mr. Franklin's death home with her. She and her parents had a very quiet dinner that evening, as silence was how her father dealt with loss. Her parents had known the couple far better than Angie did. She knew that they counted them among their friends, and her father still felt that he owed the Franklins something for the loan that had gotten his diner started, even though he had paid it back long ago. After dinner, her father got out an old bottle of wine and he and her mother began reminiscing. Angie went to bed that night wondering why she felt so upset about the death of a man that she had barely known. Chatting with him and his wife over a handful of Tuesdays hadn't opened more than a small window into their lives, but she felt his loss keenly. She supposed it must just be part of living in such a small town. Everyone knew everyone else, and any loss would be felt.

While she was on her way to the diner the next morning, her cell phone rang. She answered it, putting it on speakerphone and setting it on the dashboard. The old truck she was driving didn't have Bluetooth, which was more irritating than she could have imagined.

"Hey, Angie."

"Hey, Malcolm," she said. "What are you doing up so early?"

"I'm actually heading down to Anchorage," he said. "I left a few minutes after you did. I saw you on the road ahead of me for a while. I was just waiting until

I got somewhere with good enough cell service to call you."

"Oh. Is everything all right?" She knew his children and his ex-wife lived in Anchorage. She couldn't think of any other reason why he would be driving down there first thing on a Friday morning.

"They're fine," he said. "Well, the kids are. My ex got into a car accident last night and phoned me late last night asking if I could take the kids earlier today instead of late this evening like usual. I'm sorry, I'm going to have to cancel our dinner date for tonight."

"Of course, that's perfectly fine," she said. "I hope your ex is all right." Her voice shook a little with the last words. Car accidents weren't something that she handled well.

"She's going to be fine," Malcolm said. "She's just a bit banged up, and has a mild concussion. She doesn't want to have the kids alone this weekend in case something happens. The doctors think she'll make a full recovery, though."

"Good, I'm glad," Angie said.

She had never met Malcolm's ex-wife. That was far in the future, if it happened at all. He didn't talk about her much, and she didn't ask. From what she knew, the two of them didn't talk much, but they managed to communicate decently when it came to the kids. While she was curious about the other woman, she wasn't sure how to ask the questions she had without coming off like she was jealous or possessive, which she definitely wasn't. She'd never dated a divorced man before, so this was new territory for her.

"Can we reschedule for sometime early next week?" he asked. "I feel bad about this."

"Seriously, don't worry about it," she said. "I'm seeing Maggie Saturday, I'm going to a funeral with my parents Sunday, and I've had a busy week. I have no complaints about just staying home and reading this evening."

"Whose funeral is it?" he asked, concern laced in his voice. "Anyone I know?"

"It's Phil Franklin," she said. "I would be surprised if you knew them. They were regulars at the diner, but other than that I don't think you would have crossed paths with them."

"Yeah, I don't recognize the name," he said. "That doesn't mean I haven't run into them, of course. This town is tiny."

She chuckled. "That it is."

"So, was it both of them?"

"No, just the husband," she said. "The obituary said he passed of natural causes. I didn't know them super well, but they came in to the diner every single Tuesday morning. We will miss him. I feel so bad for his wife and his granddaughter. The granddaughter had just come to stay with them for a couple of months. He actually passed away Tuesday evening, and I saw him just earlier that day. I'm sorry, something about it is just really unsettling for me. I don't handle death well."

"Does anyone?" he asked. "I'm here if you need to talk, Angie. And I'm really sorry about what happened. Let me know if there's anything I can do. I would go to the funeral with you, but the kids –"

"It's all right," she said. "Like I said, I'm going with my parents. My dad knew them really well. He got his start up loan from them, and they've stayed pretty close ever since. He sent them Christmas cards and everything."

"I'll call later today to give your father my condolences," he said. "I should get going now. I've got to focus on driving. All that rain yesterday seems to have frozen overnight and the roads aren't that great."

"Right, I should get going too. Call me this evening once you're settled in with the kids, we can talk more if you want. Have a safe drive."

"Thanks," he said. "I'll call you later."

They said their goodbyes and Angie ended the call. By then, she was almost to the edge of town and didn't have much further to go before she reached the diner. She was glad that she didn't have to work the weekend, even though it meant that she wouldn't be able to see Malcolm or his kids Saturday morning when they came in for their weekly pancakes. It had been a long, busy, and stressful week, and she was ready for it to be over. With any luck, next week would be better.

5

Angie was up before dawn Sunday morning even though the funeral wasn't until eleven, thanks to her now well ingrained habit of waking up bright and early – or dark and early as the case may be – for the diner. Her father was also a naturally early riser and was already puttering around in the kitchen by the time she went downstairs.

"Your mother is still asleep," he said. "I'm going to head out and tend to the dogs. Do you want to come with me? I wouldn't mind the company."

"Sure," Angie said. "I'll join you in a minute, I just need some coffee first."

She drank coffee then tugged on a warm coat and slipped her bare feet into rain boots while Petunia, the elderly red and white husky that lived inside and was happily spoiled in her retirement, finished her breakfast. When she was ready to go outside, she clicked her tongue and the dog came trotting over.

"Let's see your teammates, Petunia," Angie said. "You can go say hi to everyone."

While Petunia ate kibble, the working sled dogs ate mostly raw meat and a variety of supplements. The food was prepared by hand, a laborious process that her father did every couple of weeks. The mix of raw meat, raw eggs, bone, and organ was a high energy, nutritious diet. In some of the longer races, the dogs could burn over ten thousand calories a day, and kibble just would not cut it in those situations.

Petunia led the way, running to the fenced-in dog

yard and waiting by the gate for Angie to open it. Inside the dog yard, each of the huskies had a tether spot of their own. They all had raised dog houses, which were stuffed full of clean straw, and their own food and water bowls. The yard was clear of brush and rocks, a precaution so that no dogs would be able to get their chain tangled up on anything. The tether spots gave the dogs a lot more room than a kennel would, and the trees bordering the yard gave them natural shade.

Her father had already started on feeding the dogs. He had a metal cart, which was stacked full of food bowls, that he dragged along behind him. Every time he reached the dogs, he would pick up the empty food bowl off the ground and exchange it with one that was full of meat. The dogs that had already been fed were happily digging into their meals, and the ones that were still waiting their turn were bouncing around at the ends of their chains, excitement turning even the older ones into puppies.

Angie decided to make herself useful and followed

along behind her father, gathering up water dishes. She emptied them out and stacked them together before placing them on the cart. She knew her father's routine well; once all of the dogs had been fed, he would return to the barn and clean all of the bowls he had just gathered. He would then fill the clean bowls with fresh water and head back out to hand them out to the dogs. After that, he would spend as much time as it took to clean up the messes in the dog yard and make sure the straw and all of the dog houses were dry and clean.

Caring for all of the dogs was a full-time job. Angie considered herself a dog person, but she didn't have the level of dedication that her father did. One dog was enough for her. She couldn't imagine ever wanting to have over twenty dogs to care for.

"Thanks, Angie," her father said. "I've got it from here. You can head back in if you want."

"All right, if you're sure you don't want any more

help, I'll probably go start on breakfast. Are you going to take the dogs out later today?"

"It depends on when we get back from town," he said. "I'd like to take Oracle and some of the yearlings out today."

There wasn't enough snow left on the ground to use a sled, but her father had an old ATV that the dogs could pull. Depending on how many dogs he was running, he could either put it in neutral and let them pull it themselves, or he could help them along with the motor. It was a good way to exercise a lot of dogs at once, since the ATV was a lot heavier and more solid than a sled, and he was a lot less likely to lose control.

"The dogs are going to get covered in mud," she pointed out.

"They're going to get covered in mud hanging out

here, too," he said with a shrug. "It's that time of year. You can't so much as look outside without splashing mud on something you'd rather had stayed clean."

"Well, I may not want to go on a run with the dogs in this weather, but I'll help you hook them up if you want. I don't have any plans this afternoon once the funeral is over, so let me know if you need help with any chores."

"I will, thanks Angie," he said.

Angie called Petunia to her and left the dog yard, heading back into the house. She was still wearing her pajamas and didn't bother changing before she went into the kitchen, peeking into the fridge and cupboard to find inspiration for breakfast. She settled on eggs fried sunny side up, the last of the frozen sausage patties she found in the freezer, and sliced and sugared grapefruit. It wasn't a particularly heavy meal, but they would be eating after the funeral anyway.

She had just put the sausages on when her mother made an appearance. She moved slowly, leaning heavily on her walker, her hand shaking when she reached up to brush a lock of hair out of her face. Her mother had Parkinson's disease, and it had worsened shockingly quickly. The diagnosis had surprised Angie, and was the main reason she had come back home. She had missed a lot of time with her mother in the ten years she had avoided Lost Bay, and desperately wanted to make some of it up now.

"Hey, Mom," Angie said. "How did you sleep?"

"Not too badly," the older woman said.

"I've got some sausage and eggs frying, and I was just

about to slice grapefruit. Dad made coffee when he got up, I can get you a cup if you would like."

"I can get it," her mother said in her soft voice.

"I really don't mind," Angie said. "Why don't you sit down? I'll get the creamer out too."

"Oh, all right," the older woman said. "You're going to spoil me, Angie."

She took a seat at the table, carefully moving her walker out of the way. Angie grabbed a mug out of the cupboard, poured coffee inside of it, and placed it along with the creamer and the bowl of sugar on the table in front of her mother.

"Order up," she joked.

The two of them chatted while Angie finished making breakfast. *This is certainly a lot nicer than scarfing down a bowl of instant oatmeal before I go to work*, she thought as she flipped the sausage patties over.

Her father came in through the front door, making his way to the sink to wash his hands. As he dried them, he peered over Angie's shoulder at the patties.

"We should have had you move in years ago," he said. "It's like having a live-in chef."

"Don't you dare start taking my cooking for granted," she said, pointing the spatula at him. "I'm not your maid."

It was all in good fun. Her father did a good amount of the cooking himself. He shared Angie's love for the kitchen, in fact, he was more passionate about food than she was. Even if she offered to make every single meal, he wouldn't let her. Cooking was his art.

He set the table while she finished up breakfast. She put the eggs and sausages on a serving plate and arranged the grapefruit in a bowl.

"Bon appétit," she said, carrying the food to the table. The three of them ate mostly in silence, but it was a comfortable one. Angie could almost forget that they were going to lay a family friend to rest later that day.

The funeral was being held at the town's only funeral home, and the parking lot was packed.

"Everyone knew the Franklins," her mother said softly as Angie helped her set up her walker outside the car. "He's really going to be missed. Look at how many people turned up."

"Their family has been here for decades," Angie said. "I'm not surprised that they're well-known. I just feel bad for his wife and his family. This is probably one of the hardest things they'll ever have to do."

"Speaking of his wife, I was thinking about buying the ingredients for a casserole. It might be nice to give one to Shirley. I doubt she's felt much like cooking recently."

"Of course, Mom," Angie said.

"Maybe it would be better to invite them to dinner," her father said. "Show them we really care."

They entered the funeral home and took seats near the back and Angie had time to look around the room. She was surprised at the number of faces that she recognized, even if she couldn't come up with names to match them. Mr. Franklin's wife was sitting in the front, and she saw Madison sitting next to her. It was an open casket service, but Angie felt no desire to view the body herself. She stayed seated while other people paid their respects at the casket.

It wasn't long before the service began. Angie listened as the people closest to Mr. Franklin spoke about his life and experiences. It was different from her sister's funeral. That had been full of sadness for a life not yet lived. This one was celebrating a life that had been lived to its fullest. Even his friend, Ronald, who had attended every single Tuesday breakfast at the diner with the Franklins, managed to get through his eulogy without shedding a tear.

By the time the service was over, she was glad that she had gone. Her mother and father, who knew quite a few of the people in the room, took the time to socialize once the funeral ended. Angie wandered around, feeling a bit aimless. While she recognized a lot of the people here, she didn't really know anyone personally or well. Eventually she found her way to the bathroom, and decided to use the facilities before they headed home. No sooner had she gotten into the stall when the bathroom door opened, and someone walked in. The person was on the phone, and Angie could place the voice. It was Madison, Mr. Franklin's granddaughter.

"I can't believe we are burying him today," she was saying. "My grandmother says the will should be read sometime next week. It's all moving so quickly. I can't wait to see what he left me. To be honest, I kind of forgot how much money they had until I came up here to visit them." There was a silence as whoever was on the other line spoke. "Yeah, I guess it's a good thing. If I inherited the money before I turned eighteen, my mother probably would've found a way to weasel it away from me. Look, I've got to go. I'll text you later. We're going to have to drive out to the cemetery soon and I've got to go to the bathroom first."

Madison hung up the phone and stepped into the

stall next to Angie. Angie cleared her throat, shifting around enough that Madison would know that she was there. She heard the younger woman jump.

"Sorry, I had no idea someone else was in here," she said through the stall. "I swear, you almost gave me a heart attack."

"Sorry," Angie called back, feeling a bit embarrassed at having eavesdropped on her again, even though this time she truly hadn't meant to. "I was just on my way out."

She quickly finished up in the bathroom, touching up her lipstick and fixing her hair before she left the room. She was relieved to find her mother and father waiting near the front door when she got out. The conversation she had overheard with Madison had left her feeling unsettled. She knew she had no right to judge how other people grieved, and by the sound of it, Madison had hardly known her grandfather, but something about the lack of compassion and sadness in the young woman's voice and words had rubbed her the wrong way.

6

After the funeral, Angie and her family went out to eat a late lunch. That evening, she made sure to spend quality time with both of her parents. Funerals weren't easy for any of them, and it was nice to be able to take comfort in each other. She even sent an email out to her brother, telling him what had happened and asking how he was doing.

By Monday morning, Angie had mostly put Mr. Franklin's death out of her mind. She had a job to focus on, after all, and had a busy week waiting for her. Lost Bay might be a small town, but somehow, there was no shortage of things to do.

It wasn't until she got to the diner on Tuesday morning that she was forcefully reminded of Mr. Franklin's death. Normally, she would be serving the three regulars their breakfast in just a couple hours, but she realized that she would never do that again. She didn't know if his family would be coming in this morning, and she wouldn't be surprised if they decided not to, but she certainly hoped that they would pick up the tradition again once their initial stages of grieving were over. For the first time, she was starting to see why so little had changed in the town and in the diner since she had left. There was something comforting about traditions and routines, and she didn't like this change in her routine at all.

In a stroke of luck, she was sharing this shift with Grace, the young woman who worked at the diner. Grace was cheerful and bright, and was easy to get along with. Angie liked everyone she worked with, but privately, she knew that Grace was her favorite person to share a shift with. The two of them were forming a friendship, even though Grace was quite a bit younger than Angie. She was not hard to get along with. She had known the Franklins for longer than Angie had, but somehow, she was the one who ended up comforting Angie when she found out the reason her coworker was moping about.

"He lived a good life," she said. "If I can live as long as he did and be as healthy as he was toward the end, and die a natural death, I'll be happy."

"I know you have a point," Angie said sadly. "But I still feel bad for him. And I don't think he was all there at the end."

"What do you mean?" Grace asked, looking up from where she was cleaning a pile of menus.

"The day he died, he grabbed my arm and seemed to be hallucinating," she explained. She told Grace about the people Mr. Franklin had said were following him.

"That's a bit creepy," Grace said with a shudder. "I guess maybe he wasn't all there at the end. But still, he didn't have a bad life at all. He would always tell me stories whenever I waited the table. I don't think I learned more about any other customer than him."

Angie gave a small chuckle. "Yes, the Franklins and their friend certainly love to talk. Mrs. Franklin especially. Can you do me a favor and let me know if you see them come in today? I want to offer them a meal on the house if they do."

"Of course," Grace said. "I'll come find you right away if they come in."

Despite that, Angie was mildly surprised when, a couple hours later, Grace came to find her in the kitchen. "They just walked in," she said. "They're at table three."

"Thanks," Angie said. "I'll go get their order."

As she approached the table, she examined the three guests closely. She was a bit surprised to find that Mrs. Franklin looked lighter than she had ever seen her before. Her eyes nearly sparkled as she spoke to Ronald. Ronald himself seemed a bit more animated than usual as well. He was usually the quieter of the three of them, but right now he was talking and gesticulating, a grin on his face.

Madison was the only one who seemed the same as ever. She was sitting in the corner of the booth and staring at her phone, frowning.

"Welcome to Lost Bay Burgers," Angie said as she approached their table. She set the menus down in front of them. "Anything the three of you want to order today will be on the house. You have our condolences."

"Oh, dear, thank you so much," Mrs. Franklin said.

"That means a lot to me. I know Phil always loved this place, and he was also proud of the fact that he helped it become a reality. I thought about not coming today, but then I realized it is what he would've wanted."

"Well, for what it's worth, I'm happy you came in. You three have been loyal customers for years, and I know my father really appreciates everything your husband did for him."

"Oh, I know. Your father is such a sweetheart. Did he tell you he invited us over for dinner? I really haven't had time to cook, so I appreciate it. I just love how this town comes together in times of crisis, don't you?"

It seemed that her father moved fast. She would have to ask him when the dinner was.

"I do," she said, forcing her attention to stay on her

job. "Now, what can I get you to drink?"

She brought them their drinks, then their food. If it wasn't for the conspicuous absence of the fourth member of their party, it could have been just another Tuesday.

She waited until the plates were nearly empty to check on them again. With Madison claiming the entire far booth, Ronald and Shirley were sitting together in the one across from her. Angie faltered when she saw, under the table, Ronald's hand resting on Shirley's leg. A moment later, he moved it, and she wondered if she had actually seen what she thought she had seen. Was something going on there? Was there history she wasn't aware of? Was Mr. Franklin's death maybe not such a bad thing to these people as she had thought?

She quickly shook off the thoughts, hurrying the rest of the way to the table. "Thanks for stopping in today," she said. "I hope the next few weeks pass by quickly for you."

"Oh, I'm sure they will," Shirley said. "Will I see you at dinner with your parents, Angie?"

"I'm sure I'll be there."

"Then I'll see you this weekend. Thank you again for today. It really means a lot. You have a nice afternoon."

"You, too."

Angie shot the three of them one last, forced smile then got out of there as quickly as she could. The more time she spent around Mr. Franklin's family, the more she got the sense that something was deeply off about all of them.

7

Angie was kept on her toes for the rest of the day, leaving her without much time to think. She had brought her nicer clothes with her and when her shift ended, she changed in the diner's bathroom, leaning across the sink and using the mirror to fix her hair and her makeup. She wasn't sure whether the date was an early dinner or late lunch, but it didn't really matter. She was hungry, and there would be good food. Just then, that was about the only thing that seemed important.

Malcolm was there to pick her up right on the dot. She waved to him through the window when she saw him pull into the diner's parking lot. She slid her coat over her shoulders and stepped out the door just as he parked the car.

"The diner must have really stepped up its dress code," he said when he saw her.

She grinned at him. "Yep, now all employees have to wear formal attire whenever they are on their shift. We're trying for a more upscale feel."

He chuckled and pulled her into a hug. "How are you doing? I'm so sorry that I didn't get to see you this weekend."

"I'm doing well," she said. "How are you?"

"Same as usual," he said. "The kids and I had a nice weekend, even if they were a bit worried about their mom."

"That's right. How is she doing?"

"She didn't have any issues at all this weekend, and she said she was feeling well enough to take the kids back at her usual time Sunday night. As far as I know, she's fine. Other than the fact that she is still worried about her car, of course. It was totaled. Getting a new one is going to set her back."

"It sounds like she got lucky," Angie said with a shiver.

"I know, I'm glad she's all right." He turned toward his car. "Shall we get going? We are supposed to be on a date, talking about my ex-wife probably isn't the ideal way to spend it."

Options for food in Lost Bay were a bit limited. There was the diner, of course, and Frozen Grounds, though Angie wasn't sure a coffee shop counted as a restaurant, and a small bakery inside the town limits.

The only other option was a good twenty minutes drive down the main road out of town. The steak-house was the place to go for anyone who wanted a nice meal. Even though it could have been the dictionary definition for in the middle of nowhere, it somehow always seemed to have a thriving business. It probably helped that it was the nicest restaurant for miles around. In fact, if Angie were to get technical about it, it was the only restaurant for miles around. It was nearly half-an-hour from any town, and was the only place nearby that sold food of any sort.

Even on a Tuesday afternoon, the restaurant had a few other patrons there besides Angie and Malcolm. Still, they got their pick of tables and they settled on a high top near the bar, since it was just the two of them. Angie looked over the menu, not quite sure what she wanted to get. She was hungry enough that everything sounded good.

"I think I'm going to go with a Buffalo blue cheese-burger this time," Malcolm said. "And bottomless steak fries, of course."

"I don't know what to get," Angie said. "Everything looks delicious and I'm starving. I don't know what to choose."

"They have a new Angus and shrimp option," he said. "A nice steak and seafood. That sounds hard to beat."

She looked at the menu description and nodded. It looked like it would hit the spot. A tender sirloin steak served with garlic shrimp in a butter sauce. Just reading about it made her mouth water.

She opted for that, with a side of asparagus and hollandaise sauce and sautéed squash. Since both of them had skipped lunch and were half starved, they ordered fried calamari as an appetizer, and it was brought out quickly.

"I don't know how they make their fried foods so good," Angie said as she dabbed at the dipping sauce provided with a piece of calamari. "I swear, it's better than ours at the diner. If we could figure out their recipe, we'd get a serious leg up. Even if we can't figure out just how they deep fry food to perfection, maybe I can convince my dad to start serving calamari. This is amazing."

"Didn't you say the menu has hardly changed at all over the years?"

She nodded. "My dad pretty much only makes changes when he has to. We've got a lot of the same appliances, the same food, the same suppliers, and even a lot of the same customers."

"Oh, that reminds me, how was the funeral? I still need to give your father my condolences. This weekend was just so busy."

"Yeah, my dad is taking it pretty hard. He invited the man's family over for dinner. He seems more upset about it then Mr. Franklin's wife, best friend, and granddaughter are combined."

Malcolm raised an eyebrow. "What do you mean?"

Angie looked around, making sure that no one was in easy hearing distance. Gossip spread like wildfire here.

"Well, I saw Mr. Franklin's granddaughter at the funeral. She was on the phone in the bathroom..." She told him all about the phone conversation she had overheard, and then segued into the strangely happy scene at the diner earlier that day. "It just seems weird, doesn't it? None of them really seem to care he's gone."

"Just because they don't express their grief in the

same way you do, it doesn't mean that they aren't grieving."

"But this isn't them just not expressing grief. They seem actively happy. And did I tell you that I saw Ronald – that's Mr. Franklin's friend, he eats at the diner with them a lot – put his hand on Mrs. Franklin's leg? And she was laughing. I swear, she looked ten years younger. And Madison, all she can talk about is the money she's going to inherit. For all we know, one of them pushed him down the stairs."

"Is that how he died?"

Angie waved her hand dismissively. "Well, no. I don't actually know how he died. I'm just saying, what if one of them decided to get rid of him for some reason? After what I saw these past couple of days, I almost wouldn't be surprised."

"What would the point be, though? And why now?

The poor man was old. I think it's more likely he just passed away from an illness or an accident and that's that."

"It just seems strange," Angie said with a sigh. "I'm being paranoid, aren't I?"

"Maybe a little," he said, giving her a grin. "I think the real problem is that this town is getting to you. You're starting to have a real head for gossip."

She rolled her eyes but grinned back at him. She enjoyed the fact that their relationship could be lighthearted and a bit teasing, even though on occasion she wanted things to move faster. When their knees brushed under the table, she felt her heart speed up, and when he passed her a napkin and their fingers brushed, she could have sworn that she felt a spark leap between them.

They were eating dessert when Angie's phone rang.

She pulled it out of her purse and looked at the caller ID. She was surprised to see it was from Betty.

"I'd better get this," she said apologetically to Malcolm. "I don't think Betty would call unless it was important. As a matter of fact, I don't think she's ever called me before."

"Go ahead," Malcolm said. "I hope everything's all right."

She slid her finger across the screen to answer the call, then pressed the phone to her ear. "Hello?"

"Am I speaking with Angie?"

"That's me," she said. "Is everything all right, Betty?"

"I'm fine, sorry if I concerned you. I just heard from

Shirley, though. She called me practically in tears. She said that she and her granddaughter just came from the will reading, and she found out that her husband left almost everything to their granddaughter. His sister, Zelda, is contesting the will. Poor Shirley just can't deal with it on top of everything else. I was wondering if you could put me in touch with that lawyer who helped with your sister's case."

"I don't have the number myself, that was over ten years ago, but I'll see if I can get it from my mom or dad. Not that I'm complaining, but why didn't you just call my father?"

"You know how he gets whenever your sister is mentioned. I'm sorry for asking, but I don't really know anyone else who has needed a lawyer."

"It's fine, I'll ask about it tonight."

"Thank you," Betty said. "I'll see you bright and early tomorrow morning."

"See you then."

She hung up the phone and slid it back into her purse, meeting Malcolm's raised eyebrows. "Is everything all right?"

"Just some drama with the will reading, apparently," Angie said. "He left everything to his granddaughter, and one of his other relatives is planning on contesting the will. Betty just needed a lawyer's phone number for her friend."

"The plot thickens," he said, tapping his fingers on his glass. "I'm not saying you're right, but I am saying there's a possibility. Maybe there is more to his death than it seemed."

8

It turned out that even for Angie's mother, a phone number from a decade beforehand was not easy to find. It was past midday before Angie felt her phone buzz in her pocket. She was in the middle of trimming a steak and had to ignore the call until she got a chance to return it only a few minutes before her shift ended.

She wrote down the number her mother gave her, then went out into the dining area to find Betty.

"Here you go," Angie said. "My mom said she's not sure if he's still working, but if he is, he's one of the best lawyers in the area." Betty took the paper gratefully.

"Like I said, I'm really sorry that I bothered you about this," the older woman said. "It's just poor Shirley was so distraught when she learned that Zelda was contesting the will. I just had to do what I could to help."

"I hope it gets straightened out," Angie said. "It doesn't seem fair to poor Mr. Franklin to contest his will after his death."

"Are you talking about my grandfather?"

Angie jumped. She hadn't even realized that someone was standing behind her, let alone that it was Madison. Not sure what to say, Angie froze in place. Thankfully, Betty took over.

"Yes, dear," the older woman said. "You know your Aunt Zelda is contesting the will. I was just asking Angie for the name and number of a lawyer who might be willing to help your grandmother out."

"Oh," Madison said. She looked more lost than Angie had ever seen her look. She felt a surge of pity. She really was just a teenage girl. Eighteen was barely an adult, and it certainly wasn't an age that was easy for anyone. "I see."

"Why don't you go sit down, dear? I'll bring something out for you to drink." Betty bustled away, leaving Madison to stare at Angie.

"So, I guess everyone in this town is involved with my family's drama," she said at last.

Angie flushed. "Sorry. I know it must seem like it, but it really isn't that bad. I was honestly just helping Betty out."

"I don't mind," Madison said with a shrug. "It's not like this place is my home or anything. It's just, I…" She trailed off, biting her lip.

"What is it?" Angie asked. "I know I'm just the lady who serves waffles at the diner, but I like to think I'm actually pretty helpful. If you need a friendly ear to listen to you, I'm here."

"I kind of do want to talk about something, but could we do it somewhere else? Betty seems really nice and everything and I know my grandmother trusts her, but I kind of don't want this getting out at all."

"Sure. I've only got a few minutes left in my shift. Would you like to go get coffee?"

"That would be perfect," the younger woman said.

Madison waited in the diner until Angie finished with her shift. Angie walked out to the parking lot with her.

"My truck is the really old one," she said. "I can give you a ride. Um, would your grandmother be okay with that?"

The younger woman rolled her eyes. "I'm eighteen, I'm not a kid. I don't need my grandmother's permission to get a ride to the coffee shop." She hopped into the passenger side of the vehicle before Angie could say anything else. Deciding that it was probably smarter to pick her battles, Angie shrugged and got into her side of the vehicle. She started the engine and drove the short distance to the coffee shop.

They ordered their drinks – Angie paid – and went to set down at a private table in the corner. Madison had gotten a double mocha latte with cinnamon and whipped cream, and it smelled quite a bit better than Angie's normal vanilla drink. She made a mental note to branch out a bit more next time she stopped at the coffee shop.

"The one good thing this town has is its coffee," the younger woman said. "I don't know if I could survive without this place."

"It wasn't here when I was growing up," Angie said. "I think I would have gotten hooked on caffeine at a much younger age if it was. Anyway, what was it you wanted to talk about?"

"It's about my grandfather and the will," Madison said. She bit her lip, keeping her voice low. "He... He told me he thought that someone was trying to kill him."

The words raised goosebumps on Angie's skin. She

remembered the last encounter she had with the man in the diner. "Did he talk about people following him and watching him? People who weren't really there?"

The younger woman nodded; her eyes wide. "How did you know that?"

"He said something similar to me. I didn't take him seriously. Maybe I should have –"

"I don't think someone actually killed him," Madison said, some of her old attitude coming back. "I think he was going crazy, and I'm worried that it might sway the lawyers into giving my aunt what she wants. I was reading up about the stuff online, and if they can prove that he wasn't in his right mind when he made the will, they can invalidate it. If people find out that he was seeing things that weren't there, it could wreck everything. I don't know what to do."

"Do you know when he changed the will? And did he leave absolutely everything to you? I only know what Betty told me, and that wasn't much."

"I've got no idea when he changed it," Madison said. "And he left almost everything to me, but he left my grandmother enough for her to be comfortable. He also left her a lot of old things that I am not really interested in and I don't care about. We're the only two people who got anything."

"Well, I know I said that I would be a friendly ear to listen, but when I said that I was also really hoping I could give you advice or something. Unfortunately, I don't really know anything about this. I guess I would just suggest that you go talk to the lawyer whose number I gave Betty. He could probably find out when the will was last changed, and you could tell him your concerns.

"This is all so stressful. I wish my aunt would just butt out."

"Do you know if they had a fight or something? I am just wondering why he didn't leave her anything."

"I've got no idea," Madison said. "All my mom ever said about it was that the two of them had a fight years and years ago and haven't talked since. This is my dad's side of the family, and I don't see him much so I don't really know that much about them. Why? You think it's important?"

"I have no idea," Angie said honestly. "All of this stuff is above my head. But I do hope that everything gets resolved and that everyone is as happy as possible about what happens. Your poor grandmother has already been through a lot. She doesn't need to suffer any more."

9

Angie could not dismiss the theory that she was going crazy. She thought about poor Mr. Franklin and his somewhat strange family the entire drive home. Try as she might, she couldn't pinpoint exactly what bothered her so much about the whole situation. If any one of the things that made her uncomfortable was taken on its own, she would have simply shrugged it off and moved on with her life. However, all of them together raised red flags. Mr. Franklin's strange behavior the day that he died, the unusually cheerful way that the people closest to him seemed to be acting after his death, and the entire mess with his granddaughter, the will, and the unhappy sister. Angie was convinced that there was something going on, but the only problem was, she was at a loss as to how to figure out what.

The house was empty when she got home. Her father had replaced her at work, and her mother had left a note on the kitchen table saying that she had gone out with Cheryl, their neighbor, for a trip into town. It was rare that Angie had the house to herself, and she decided to take advantage of it by pouring herself a cup of tea and taking a nice relaxing hot bath.

That was the plan, anyway. She was settled in the tub, enjoying the smell of the bubblebath and the feel of the hot water cradling her, when she picked up her phone with the intention to check her emails. She didn't even make it to the email application before a news story popped up, catching her eye.

Teen girl inherits over one million dollars from grandfather.

She clicked the headline, already knowing what she was going to find. Madison was pictured, what looked like a senior picture from her high school yearbook. Her grandfather and grandmother were both named in the story. The article mentioned the man's death and actually told Angie more than the obituary had. He had suffered a heart attack after a long mental and physical decline. According to the paper, his death hadn't come as a surprise to anyone. She begged to differ.

The paper also had a mention that the will was being contested. It didn't say by whom, but she was sure that would come out, eventually. Angie's first thought was to wonder just what their story being picked up by the local news sites would do to their family. It would only make what was already a bad situation worse.

She pinched the phone screen to zoom in on one of the photos in the article. It was a picture of Zelda, who was listed as one of the people who had survived him and who had been hoping to be named in the will, though the news article didn't outright say that she was the one who was challenging it.

What caught Angie's eye the most was the woman's face. She looked familiar. She was the same woman Angie had spoken to on Thursday at the diner, who had asked for hotel recommendations.

Angie frowned at the picture, trying to connect the dots in her mind. The woman had been asking for hotel recommendations, because the motel she had been staying at since Monday was unsatisfactory.

That meant that the woman, Mr. Franklin's sister, had been in town since before her brother's death. Why hadn't she joined them Tuesday for breakfast? Had she been at the funeral? Was she still in town? Angie had no idea. She didn't remember seeing her at the funeral, but there had been a lot of people there, and she of course hadn't been looking for her.

Petunia began to bark on the other side of the bath-room door and Angie jumped. Her tea was luke-warm now, and the bathwater was beginning to cool off as well. She put her phone down and drained the tub. By the time she had dried off and dressed, and had gone down the hallway to the front door to see what all the commotion was, Cheryl was saying goodbye to Angie's mother. She gave Angie a curt nod, and she nodded back. The two of them had had a strained relationship ever since Cheryl's husband had been convicted of murder. Angie had been the one to uncover the crime, and Cheryl seemed to blame her personally for the entire fiasco. However, she had kept up her friendship with Angie's mother throughout it all, so Angie did her best to keep things polite in turn.

Cheryl left, shutting the front door behind her, and Angie had the chance to greet her mother. "I have groceries in the kitchen," the older woman said. "Cheryl brought them in for me."

She felt a rush of gratitude toward the older woman.

Murderous husband or not, Cheryl was a good friend to her mother.

"I'll help you put them away," Angie offered. They began walking toward the kitchen.

"How was your day?" her mother asked.

"It was stressful," Angie admitted.

"If you had such a hard day, you should go lie down. The groceries can wait for your father, the ones I can't do myself anyway."

"It will only take a couple of minutes," Angie said as they stepped into the kitchen. She grabbed a carton of milk and put it in the fridge. "Speaking of Dad, though, do you know what time he's supposed to be home?"

"You would know better than I would. I'm sure he has his schedule written down at the diner. Though I suppose he usually stays late, so that probably wouldn't help you much. He'll call if he'll be home past dinnertime. Did you need something from him?"

"I just wanted to ask him something," Angie said. "It can wait, though. Do you have something planned for dinner? I'll get started on it in a little bit if you'd like. I don't really have any other plans for today, and I don't think I'll be able to focus on a book or a movie right now."

"The recipe is by the microwave," her mother said. "I bought the ingredients for blackened chicken with a creamy wild rice side dish. You don't have to cook though, dear. You do that all day at work."

"Mom, most of the reason I moved here was to help you," Angie said. "Trust me, I really don't mind at all." She put a couple boxes of cereal in the cupboard. "You're supposed to be resting and taking care of yourself."

"I just hate feeling lazy," her mother said, lowering herself into a kitchen chair.

"You're not lazy if you listen to your body's physical limitations," Angie said. "Mom, you're sick. You always took care of me when I was sick. It's my turn to take care of you. I'm happy to do all of this."

And she was. Even though she had been looking forward to having the evening off, this was even better. She wanted something to focus on, something to make her feel useful. Mr. Franklin's death was still bothering her, and she wanted to focus on her own family in an effort to forget about his.

By the time her father got home late that evening, the kitchen table was set and dinner was about to come out of the oven. For as long as Angie could remember, they had always eaten late. Her father usually got home from the diner around eight or nine, and they would have a family dinner together then. He often ate lunch at the diner, but he would wait to eat dinner with his family. Having meals together had been important to her parents during her childhood. While Angie at eighteen hadn't exactly appreciated it, she did now. It made her realize just how hard her father had worked to give them all a healthy and normal childhood.

The three of them asked the normal questions about each other's days as they began eating. The chicken was good, though blackened dishes weren't usually Angie's favorite, and the wild rice was perfect. Angie thought that the diner would benefit from adding more dishes like this. Maybe calamari was a bit off the mark, but wild rice and chicken was a great homestyle dish. She made a mental note to write up some recipe sheets for new ideas that she had and ask her dad about them. He might be resistant to change, but she wasn't, and if he wanted her to eventually take the diner over so he could retire, then he was going to have to listen to her, at least about some things.

"So, Dad," she said once they had all eaten enough to squash their hunger. "Did you see the news article about Mr. Franklin's granddaughter, and the will that is being contested?"

"I did," he said, shaking his head. "I'm devastated for his wife. All of this must be almost too much for her to deal with so soon after his death. If I'm being fair, though, I can see where his other relatives are coming from. The poor man wasn't himself in his last few months."

"What do you know about his condition?" Angie asked, curious.

"Not much," her father said. "No one did. It was one of the things he would complain to me about. He kept telling me how useless doctors were, since they couldn't figure out what was wrong with him. It was a real mystery, and I guess they didn't solve it in time."

"You think they'll be able to use his illness to override his final wishes?"

"I don't know. They may have a case. It's likely they will revert it to whatever his previous will was before the changes were made, if they do decide that he wasn't in his right mind when he updated it."

"That would be a shame for his granddaughter."

Her father shrugged. "I'm sure she'd get a good portion of the money anyway. If I'm being honest, I was surprised when I read that she was the only one named in his will other than Shirley."

"Do you think it's possible any of his family had

something to do with his death?" she asked, trying to keep her voice neutral.

"Angie, no," her father said, sounding tired.

"What?"

"We're having his wife, his granddaughter, Ronald, and possibly other members of their family over for dinner in two days. You're an adult and you're free to have whatever crazy theories you want to, but you're not going to bring any up at dinner in front of my guests, do you understand? I'm not going to invite these people over, people whom I respect and whose friendship I value, and have you stir up all sorts of panic by accusing someone of murder. Remember what you did to the neighbors?"

"I wasn't wrong about them, though," Angie said, feeling annoyed.

"If you remember, you actually accused Cheryl. You only got lucky that one of them actually was a killer. Believe what you want, Angie, but please don't start anything at dinner."

"Fine," she said. "But I'm going to be keeping a close eye on them. Something strange is going on, and I want to find out what."

10

Dinner turned out to be a much larger affair than Angie had originally expected. Somehow, Malcolm, Maggie, Joshua, and even Cheryl all ended up being invited to their Friday night get together. It was turning into a real dinner party, and Angie would have been looking forward to it if it wasn't for her reservations about the Franklins.

She got off work at two on Friday and stopped by the grocery store to pick up a few extra ingredients that her mother had asked her to grab, along with a delicious looking cheesecake that she just couldn't resist. She messaged Maggie when she was on her way home. Her friend was planning on coming over early to help her and her mom cook. That way

Joshua would be able to play with the dogs, which he and they enjoyed greatly.

With her father busy at the diner until just before dinner, that left Angie and her mother in charge of getting everything ready. Even though she had a few hours before dinner was supposed to begin, she still felt rushed. Nonetheless, she took a few minutes to show Joshua how to change out the dogs' water bowls and where to put the dirty food bowls, and let him take care of changing out the bowls in the dog yard. She told him he was free to play fetch with Petunia when he was done, or to come in and join them if he got cold.

Maggie, who had spent many evenings at Angie's house when they were younger, was in the kitchen chatting away with Angie's mother when she got back inside. They both fell silent and looked up when she came in, and she wrinkled her nose at them.

"Were you talking about me? Should my ears be burning?"

"No," Maggie said, her cheeks flushing. She cleared her throat. "So, what are we making? And thanks again for inviting me, Mrs. Seaver." She directed that last toward Angie's mom.

"Of course, sweetheart," the older woman said. "You're always welcome here. Joshua too, of course. It's nice to have some life in the house again. Anytime you want to come over to eat or just chat, you're welcome. Your father must be so proud of you. You've grown up into a truly lovely young woman, and your son is such a kind and polite young man."

"I know my father loves me, but I don't think he's necessarily proud of me," Maggie said, suddenly looking a bit uncomfortable. "I mean, I am a single mom, divorced, and struggling to raise my son on my own. I think he expected better of me."

"None of that is anything to be ashamed of," Angie's mom said, touching her hand gently. "It takes a lot of strength to be a single mom. I don't know your father well enough to speak for him, but I am proud of you. Life threw you a curveball, and you're making it work. I think I know what I'm saying when I tell you that things don't always go how you had hoped. It's your attitude that matters more than anything, and every single time I see you, I'm impressed with your attitude."

Maggie gave Angie's mother a small smile. "Thanks, Mrs. Seaver. That means a lot."

"Oh, call me Anise," the other woman said. "Enough of that Mrs. Seaver stuff. You aren't a ten-year-old anymore. We are both adults, so just call me by my first name. Having an adult woman call me Mrs. Seaver just makes me feel old."

"Well, that's the last thing I want to do," Maggie said. "Anise it is."

"You'll always be Mom to me," Angie said. "I don't care how old it makes you feel."

Her mother tossed a wad of paper towel at her playfully, and Angie swooped in to kiss her cheek.

"We should get started on the ham. I want to at least have everything in the oven before Malcolm gets here. I know he's going to offer to help, and there really isn't enough room in the kitchen for all four of us to try to cook."

They had planned for a traditional spring meal of honey baked ham, cheesy scalloped potatoes that Angie was making from scratch, a creamy green bean and mushroom casserole, and fruit and coconut salad. The cheesecake would be for dessert, along with a homemade strawberry drizzle.

Cooking with Maggie and her mother was a lot of fun. Even though she was nervous about the coming dinner with the Franklins, she managed to relax and laugh with them. Joshua came in while they were working on the potatoes and helped them out cheerfully enough. He set the table, handed them spices, and chatted happily about his day while he did it. Angie smiled as she watched him.

It would be nice if Malcolm could bring his kids tonight, she found herself thinking. The thought took her by surprise. Maybe she was more ready to officially meet them than she had thought.

Malcolm showed up a few minutes early, which wasn't a surprise. He lived only a mile away, and worked from home, so he didn't have far to go. He arrived at the door bearing a gift of sparkling juices. Angie's mother didn't drink, since alcohol interfered with some of her medications, so the sparkling juices were a nice touch.

"It smells amazing in here," he said as he took off his boots and jacket. He pulled Angie into a quick hug, then did the same with her mother and shook Maggie's and Joshua's hands. "I was hungry when I headed over, but now I'm half starved. Is there anything I can do to help?"

"We are pretty much done," Angie said. "Thanks for offering, though."

"What are you making?" he asked.

Angie told him about the meal as they walked toward the kitchen. She put the sparkling juices in the fridge, then had to take them out again to make room for the fruit salad, which Maggie was just finishing up. After a few minutes creatively reorganizing the fridge, she made room for everything again. The dinner was starting to feel like a full-blown holiday celebration.

Her father arrived just minutes before the Franklins did. By then, dinner was ready, the candles on the table were lit, and a heated conversation about two of the states sports teams was underway. Angie wasn't much of a sports person herself, but Maggie and Malcolm both watched them to some extent.

They were all ready and waiting when the Franklins showed up. Angie waited at the door for them. She watched as Mrs. Franklin, Madison, Ronald, and one more person all got out of the vehicle. It wasn't until the small group got into the pool of light cast by the outdoor light that Angie realized to the fourth person was. It was Zelda, Mr. Franklin's sister.

11

The food was almost good enough to make up for all the awkwardness that saturated the dinner table. The awkwardness was centered on Zelda, the one who was contesting the will. Angie had been on the verge of asking either Madison or Mrs. Franklin what she was doing there, but had lost her nerve when she saw her father watching her. She knew that it was important to him that this dinner go well. The Franklins were an important family, both to him and to the town. She didn't want to disappoint him.

Nonetheless, there was a tangible sense of uneasiness as they settled around the table to eat. Angie was sandwiched between Malcolm and Maggie, with Joshua sitting next to his mother, followed by

Cheryl, and Angie's parents sitting at the head and foot of the table. The Franklins were seated along the opposite side of the table from Angie. The dining room table, expanded with an extra leaf, was just barely large enough to fit them all.

What is she doing here? Angie wondered. Why did they invite her? Why would she want to come?

"Mr. and Mrs. Seaver, the food is great," Madison said from where she was seated across from Angie.

"Angie and Maggie made most of it," Angie's mother said. "You can thank them."

"Well, it seems like your daughter has inherited your skills in the kitchen, Rod," Mrs. Franklin said. "Eating at the diner is one thing, but this has really sealed the deal. You know, if you ever wanted to think about opening another restaurant, I'm sure we could work something out. My husband really loved your diner, and I think he would be happy to know that some of his money was going to help you further."

Next to her, Zelda made a strangled noise. Everyone at the table turned to look at her. There was no sound except for the clinking of Joshua's fork against his plate. Angie realized for the first time just how uncomfortable this must be for Zelda. Everyone at the table knew that she was contesting her brother's will. She must know that they know. Yet for some reason, she had attended the dinner anyway.

"So, Zelda," Angie's father began. Angie shot him a look. She recognized the tone of voice he was using. It was a tone he used when a customer was irritating him, but he was being too polite to actually say anything about it. "What do you do?"

"I work in the medical field," the older woman said. "I'm quite respected in my profession."

Angie and Maggie exchanged a look. What exactly was the woman trying to convince them of?

"How nice," Angie's father continued in the same tone of voice he was using before. "Is it a highly specialized field?"

"I wouldn't say highly specialized," she replied. "I have familiarity with a broad range of medical conditions. I didn't specialize until later in my career, and I haven't forgotten my earlier training. When I was younger, I worked in the ER for a while. Trust me when I say I saw just about everything there."

Ronald dropped his fork and there was another long, awkward pause. Angie was beginning to get the feeling that there was a subtext here that she was missing. What was her father playing at? What was Zelda playing at, for that matter? None of it was making sense to her.

"Angie, your family seems nice," Madison said softly to her. Angie looked over to her, feeling a surge of pity for the young adult who was caught in the middle of her family's drama.

"They are, for the most part," she said with a small smile. "No one's perfect, of course, and I'd be lying if I said they didn't drive me crazy sometimes, but I think I'll keep them.

"I'll trade you," the young woman whispered, her lips twitching up in a half smile.

"You don't mean that," Angie said softly. "I know things are rough right now, but things will get back to normal soon."

"You have no idea," Madison said, her voice so low that Angie could barely hear it.

She frowned. Was there something else going on? Something Angie wasn't aware of? She had certainly been getting an off feeling about the entire group for a while now. She wanted to know more.

"Can I use your bathroom, Mrs. Seaver?" Madison said suddenly. She interrupted a conversation between Malcolm and Ronald.

"Of course, dear," Angie's mother said.

Madison turned to stare at Angie, her eyes widening slightly. Jumping up, Angie said, "I'll go show you where it is."

The two of them left the table and Angie led Madison through the house toward the guest bathroom that she had claimed as her own.

"It's through that door, if you actually have to go," she said.

"I don't," Madison said. "I just needed to get away from the table for a bit. I'm going insane here. This entire side of my family has just lost it. If I wasn't afraid of losing more money than me or my mom have ever seen in our entire lives, I would just take off."

"What's going on?" Angie asked.

"I walked in on my grandmother and Ronald..." She shuddered. "Kissing. It was horrible. Old people shouldn't do that."

Angie almost snorted at the young woman's tone, then realized what she was saying.

"I'm sorry. So soon after your grandfather passed...

That must have been a shock."

"No." Madison shook her head. "I saw it before he passed away. Tuesday morning, right before we left for the diner. My grandpa was busy helping me with some of my college applications, and Ronald showed up at the house since we were all going to carpool to the diner together, and he and my grandmother were alone in the kitchen, and I walked by to go to the bathroom, and I saw them. I didn't know whether I should say something to my grandfather or not, then later that day he passed away. And now they're not even pretending that they aren't involved. I didn't really know my grandfather that well, but it kind of makes me mad. I mean, from what I do know about him he was a nice guy. He really doesn't deserve this."

"I had no idea," Angie said. "That must be hard to deal with."

"That was hard, all right. It only got worse when my

Aunt Zelda showed up. I don't mean when she notified us that she was contesting the will, I mean when she showed up at the house this morning and started yelling and screeching at my grandmother for lying to her about something. She hasn't left since. She and my grandmother had a long talk in private, and I guess they came to some sort of agreement, because Aunt Zelda has been hanging around in the house like an angry vulture ever since. I just can't stand it anymore. They've all gone insane. I thought this dinner would force them to be normal, but it didn't. It's just getting worse."

"Look, I know that you don't really know me that well, but if you want to sleep in the guest room here tonight, tomorrow I can help you go find a cheap motel room to stay in. I don't think it's safe for you to stay at your grandmother's house anymore."

Madison paled. "What do you mean, it's not safe? I know they're acting weird and it is kind of freaking me out, but I never thought I was actually in danger."

Angie bit her lip. "Listen. I promised my father I wouldn't bring this up during the dinner, but I think this is too important. Keep in mind that I don't actually know for sure, so don't tell anyone, but... I think someone might have murdered your grandfather."

The young woman's eyes widened. "Who?"

"I don't know." Angie would not have accepted a million dollars right then to admit that Madison had been one of her suspects. "But if you think about it, all three of them out there have motives. Your grandmother, both for his money and to hide the fact that she was having an affair, Ronald, for similar reasons, and your Aunt Zelda, who, from what I heard, hasn't actually spoken to your grandfather for years."

"That's not true," Madison said. "About Aunt Zelda and my grandpa. He saw her Monday night. She picked him up right outside the house. I didn't know who she was then, but I recognize her now."

Angie frowned, trying to put the pieces together. Zelda had seen Mr. Franklin the day before he died. Then she had hung around town until she learned that she had inherited nothing from his will. Then she had contested the will and... Angie wasn't clear on what had happened next. The argument between her and Mrs. Franklin didn't make any sense.

Unless... What if Mrs. Franklin had been the one who had convinced her husband to change his will, and Zelda had learned of it? That could explain the argument, especially if Zelda had been hoping for money from her brother. If she worked in the medical field, like she said, she might have access to medications that would take a day to kill him. She could have poisoned him when she picked him up on Monday, and simply waited for him to die twenty-four hours later.

"Madison, I think you should stay here. I'm about to break a promise to my father. I think I know who killed your grandfather."

12

Leaving a befuddled Madison behind, Angie hurried back into the dining room and approached the table slowly. She was trying to build up courage for what she was about to do. Yes, she promised her father not to bring any of this up or cause a scene, but if she was right about the killer, then this could be a life or death situation for Madison or Mrs. Franklin. And she was right. Well, she was probably right. Everything made sense, all of the clues lined up.

"Angie?" Her father was looking at her, puzzled.

"Sorry, Dad," she said. "But I think I know how Mr. Franklin died."

reigned ?

For some reason, she had expected silence to fall. Instead, the opposite happened. There were gasps and shrieks, and someone knocked over a glass of water. The chaos only rained for a moment before people focused their attention back on her, looking expectant, frightened, and worried.

"His sister did it."

As one, they all turned to look at Zelda. The words that hardly landed before the older woman stood up and pointed her finger at Angie.

"You don't know anything, so I suggest that you shut your mouth."

"She's telling the truth," a voice from behind Angie said. She turned to see Madison standing at the entranceway to the dining room.

"It all makes sense if you think about it. Zelda and Grandpa didn't talk for years and years. Then she comes to visit him Monday night and a day later he's dead. She contested the will; she obviously thought she was getting something out of it." Madison bit her lip. "I didn't know him very well, and thanks to you, Zelda, I'll never get a chance."

"Well, I never," Zelda said. She crossed her arms in front of her chest. "I don't know how you managed it, but you somehow got everything all twisted around. I did not kill my brother. I was trying to save his life."

"If you were trying to save his life, then why did he die a day after he met you for the first time in years?" the young woman asked.

"Because Phil was always stupidly stubborn. He waited too long to ask me for help. He should have called me as soon as he knew something was wrong and the doctors failed to find out what it was. If he had done that, he may have still been alive. As it was, the poison had progressed too far, and even if I had found out what it was right away, there wouldn't have been anything I could've done."

"Okay, I'm sorry, but I'm taking Joshua and we're leaving," Maggie said, standing up suddenly. "I don't really want to believe any of this, but I have the horrible feeling that someone here is telling the truth. I'm not letting my son eat dinner with a killer."

She grabbed Joshua by the shoulders and half dragged him out of the room. No one made a move to stop them. Angie wanted to follow her friend, but couldn't miss what was happening.

"I think we should call the police," Angie's mother said softly.

"No!" Mrs. Franklin said sharply. "No police. We can handle this ourselves."

Angie's father, who had been fuming silently ever since Angie had spoken up, raised an eyebrow. "Why don't you want to call the police, Shirley?"

"Because this is a family matter, and it can be handled inside the family."

"I don't know the whole story here," Malcolm said. "But I do know enough to know that the person who doesn't want to call the police is probably the guilty one."

"Are you accusing me of killing my husband?" Mrs. Franklin asked, her voice rising up near a shriek.

"I'm not accusing anyone of anything," Malcolm said, raising his hands. "I'm just saying, telling the table you don't want to call the police looks pretty bad. I think we should call them and let them sort this out. That's what they do."

"They don't need to sort anything out," Zelda snapped. "I know exactly what happened and who did it. It's just a matter of convincing the right people. Apparently, there are some people who can be blind when it comes to the people they care about. I never had that unfortunate flaw."

"Trusting the people you love isn't a flaw," Mrs. Franklin said, glaring daggers at the other woman. "There is a reason that no one in your entire family cared enough to keep in touch with you, Zelda. It's because you are coldhearted and –"

"Enough," Angie's father snapped. "Can someone please just explain what's going on?"

"My brother was poisoned," Zelda said slowly, enunciating each word. "He was poisoned over a long period of time, going slowly insane as his body failed itself. The person who did it is in this very room."

The older woman glared around at them. Her eyes flitted across Madison, and Angie felt her pulse speed up. Had she been wrong about the younger woman?

But then her gaze moved on. Eventually, her cold eyes landed on Ronald. The man's eyes widened.

"Mercury," Zelda said. She said it with a finality that told Angie the older woman thought that explained everything.

"I don't –" Malcolm started to say, but he was interrupted by Mrs. Franklin.

"No," the woman said. "He wouldn't. You're crazy. You should be locked in the nut house. You don't know anything."

"I know the signs, Shirley," Zelda said. "Mercury poisoning isn't very common anymore. Not to this extent, anyway. Heavy long-term exposure over a period of months... It had to be someone close to him. More importantly, it had to be someone with access to Mercury. Someone who uses it every day. Someone who has tools containing mercury. Someone who would have no trouble slipping a little bit into his drink or food."

Angie stared between Zelda, who looked triumphant, and Ronald, who was beginning to fidget and who was worryingly pale. Mrs. Franklin seemed to have been struck speechless.

And all of a sudden, and she got it.

"He's an amateur weatherman," Angie said. "His tools, the things he measures temperature and barometer and all that with. They have Mercury in them. He was Phil's best friend, and he's having an affair with his wife. He did it."

"She gets it," Zelda said, with a nod in Angie's direction.

She wasn't even finished with her sentence when Ronald stood from his seat with such violence that the chair fell over backwards. He stumbled as he ran toward the hallway door, but even so he had enough of a head start that Angie's father and Malcolm, who both jumped up to chase him, couldn't catch up before he pushed his way through the front door.

They chased Ronald through the yard, but they gave up quickly. It was dark outside, and he had too much of a lead on them.

"What do we do?" Madison asked, her voice hysterical. "He's getting away. He killed my grandfather, and he's getting away."

Behind them, Mrs. Franklin was screaming and shouting into the night, alternatively cursing the man and asking him to come back. Zelda looked like she was attempting to comfort her.

"He's not going to get far," Malcolm said. "There's, what, three houses on this road? He doesn't have the keys to your family's car, and he's not going to find a ride into town."

"Maggie will have already called her father," Angie said. "I know her, she wouldn't have just gone home and left us to get murdered or something."

Madison, Malcolm, Angie, and Angie's father all turned to look in the direction Ronald had fled.

There would be nowhere he could hide in the wilds of Alaska, not for long anyway.

"They'll catch him," Angie said softly to Madison.

The younger woman gave a sharp nod. "Good."

EPILOGUE

It wasn't an easy decision to make, but in the end, Angie knew she didn't really have a choice. She pressed her pen to the paper before she could change her mind, and wrote her name four times. Four Saturdays, gone. Four weeks, with six-days sacrificed to her job.

She was working Saturday mornings for a month.

"I did it," she said.

"Really?" Malcolm's voice sounded a bit distant

through her cell phone's low-quality speakers, but still warm and happy.

"Really," she said. "I work Saturdays now. Your kids better like my pancakes better than Betty's, because that's all they're getting for a month."

"You know, you didn't have to do this."

"I know." She sighed. "I wanted to. Well, you know what I mean. I want to spend the extra time with you and get to know your kids without the pressure of them knowing about our relationship. Something about staying up with you all night while the police searched my parents' property for an escaped murderer really made me realize how much I like having you around."

"You could describe it in a more romantic way," he said, chuckling. "We stayed up together all night, tucked under blankets beneath the stars while multicolored lights strobed around us. And... well, I'm not sure how to make the escaped murderer part seem romantic. But I get what you mean. We've been through a lot together. I get the feeling that we are going to keep going through a lot together in the future. I think I'd like you to keep making the kids pancakes, even when you don't work Saturday mornings. And yes, they do like yours better than Betty's. I told you before, you do the funny faces better."

She smiled triumphantly to herself. Baby steps. For some reason, meeting a guy's kids – officially – was so much more frightening than coming face-to-face with a suspected murderer.

She was glad that the manhunt hadn't gone on past dawn. They had finally found Ronald trying to flag down a car a few miles down the road, dirty and scraped up from his mad run through the woods in the dark. He had confessed everything; the slow poisoning of his friend over a period of months after years of being in love with his wife. Angie had no doubts that he would be going to prison for a very, very long time.

She was hoping to be able to keep in touch with Madison. She had left town with her aunt to figure out what she wanted to do with her future. She had money now, thanks to what her grandfather had willed her, and she also had a new appreciation for the medical sciences. Angie hoped that she would find a path that she was passionate about. The young woman had grown on her, there is no doubt about that.

Angie said her goodbyes to Malcolm, promising to see him later that day, and slipped her phone into her pocket. It was a Monday, the first day of her first six-day work week. She had a lot of work to do, both at the diner and in her life. She still wasn't completely sure what she wanted to do with her own future, but she did know she didn't want anything to change too dramatically too fast.

She was happy where she was, and she wasn't planning on leaving anytime soon.

Book 18: A Side of Murder

Book 19: Wrapped in Murder

Book 20: Glazed Ham Murder

Book 21: Chicken Club Murder

Book 22: Pies, Lies and Murder

Book 23: Mountains, Marriage and Murder

Book 24: Shrimply Murder

Book 25: Gazpacho Murder

Book 26: Peppered with Murder

Book 27: Ravioli Soup Murder

Book 28: Thanksgiving Deli Murder

Book 29: A Season of Murder

Book 30: Valentines and Murder

Book 31: Shamrocks and Murder

Book 32: Sugar Coated Murder

Book 33: Murder, My Darling

Killer Cookie Series

Book 1: Killer Caramel Cookies

AUTHOR'S NOTE

I'd love to hear your thoughts on my books, the storylines, and anything else that you'd like to comment on—reader feedback is very important to me. My contact information, along with some other helpful links, is listed below. If you'd like to be on my list of "folks to contact" with updates, release and sales notifications, etc.... just shoot me an email and let me know. Thanks for reading!

Also...

... if you're looking for more great reads, I am proud to announce that Summer Prescott Books publishes several popular series by Cozy authors Summer Prescott and Gretchen Allen, as well as Carolyn Q. Hunter, Blair Merrin, Susie Gayle and more!

CONTACT SUMMER PRESCOTT
BOOKS PUBLISHING

Twitter: @summerprescott1

Blog and Book Catalog: http://summerprescottbooks.com

Email: summer.prescott.cozies@gmail.com

And...look up The Summer Prescott Fan Page and Summer Prescott Publishing Page on Facebook – let's be friends!

To download a free book, and sign up for our fun and exciting newsletter, which will give you opportunities to win prizes and swag, enter contests, and be the first to know about New Releases, click here: http://summerprescottbooks.com

42409048R00100